JUICE
THE PIG

To my dear long-suffering parents – Martine

First published 1996 by Macmillan Children's Books
a division of Macmillan Publishers Limited
Eccleston Place, London SW1W 9NF
and Basingstoke
Associated companies worldwide

ISBN 0 333 63850 6 (hardback)
ISBN 0 333 66663 1 (paperback)

1 3 5 7 9 8 6 4 2

A CIP catalogue record for this book
is available from the British Library

Printed and bound in Great Britain by
BPC Books Ltd
A member of
The British Printing Company Ltd

JUICE
THE PIG

Martine Oborne
Illustrated by Axel Scheffler

MACMILLAN CHILDREN'S BOOKS

Juice the Pig was very fond of hats.

He had

big hats,

small hats,

tall hats,

floppy hats,

stripy hats,

feathery hats,

and suitable-for-every-and-any-occasion sort of hats.

In fact, he had so many hats that you would need
more than all your fingers and toes to count them.

When Juice the Pig's mum saw Juice messing about in his hats, she worried. "Juicy," she would say, "you are a Very Vain Little Pig and I do not know what is to become of you. You have many lessons to learn in life and you will learn none of them from hats!"

But Juice did not listen. He was too busy

tipping

and cocking,

raising

and straightening,

and doing all the other things you do with hats.

One day, Juice the Pig
was out and about when
he bumped into a giraffe.
Juice was wearing a
tall, teetering, high-as-
a-chimney sort of hat.
"My hat makes me
almost as tall as
you!" he cried
proudly to
the giraffe.

The giraffe snorted and with one fell swoooop

snatched up the hat   and flipped it onto his head.

"Mmmmm, indeed,
a very fine hat,
drawled the giraffe.
"I should like to
keep it for myself,"
he continued,
ignoring the hot,
cross piglet below.

"But if you are really determined to get your hat back, you
must climb up my long, long neck to get it."
Juice looked up at the giraffe's long, long legs and his long,
long neck.

It is not easy for little pigs to climb, but Juice did want his hat back and so he decided to do it.

It was **horrid**. The giraffe kept wriggling his neck because, he said, Juicy was so tickly.

But Juice was **determined** and so, at last, he got his hat.

"Wheeeee!" he said as he slid down the back of the giraffe's neck and bomped onto the ground. "I am a Very **Determined** Pig and I Have My Hat!"

The next day, Juice the Pig was out and about when he stumbled over a crocodile.

Juice was wearing a fierce, pointy, snap-your-tail-off sort of hat. "My hat makes me almost as fierce as you!" he cried proudly to the crocodile.

The crocodile yawned

and with a quick slurpety-slurp

snaffled the hat deep inside his mouth.

"Mmmmm, indeed, a very gobblesome hat. I should like to eat it for my dinner," drooled the crocodile, ignoring the raging pink piglet. "But if you are really **brave** enough to get your hat back, you must come inside my hungry, hungry jaws to get it."

Juice looked at
the crocodile's  hungry, hungry
lips  and its hungry,
hungry jaws.

It is not easy for little pigs to jump inside a crocodile's mouth,
but Juice did want his hat back and so he decided to do it.

It was **terrifying**. The crocodile kept licking his lips because,
he said, Juicy was so tasty, but Juicy was **brave** and so, at last,
he got his hat.

"Hurrah!" he shouted as he leapt off the crocodile's tongue and ran off as fast as he could. "I am a Very Determined **and Brave** Pig and I Have My Hat!

The next day, Juice the Pig was out and about when he became surrounded by a band of monkeys.

Juice was wearing a round, bouncy, let's-play-catch sort of hat. "My hat makes me almost as playful as you!" he cried proudly to the band of monkeys.

The monkeys yahooed
and with a quick flick
of the tail . . .

. . . one swiped the
hat and threw it
to his friend.

"Mmmmm, indeed, a very fun hat. We should like to play with it every day," cried the monkeys, ignoring the angry piggy in the middle.

"But if you are **patient**, you can have it back when we are finished."

Juice looked at how the monkeys threw his hat high, high into the air. It is not easy for little pigs to be patient, but Juice did want his hat back and so he decided to do it.

Poor Juice. It was **boring**.

The monkeys played for hours because, they said, it was such fun teasing Juicy.

But Juice was **patient** and so, in the end, he got his hat.

"At last!" he sighed as he said
goodbye to the monkeys and
plodded off. "I am a Very
Determined, Brave
and Patient Pig
and I Have My Hat!"

The next day,
it was cold. Juice the
Pig was out and about as
usual when he spied a tiny
mouse. Juice was wearing a soft,
teeny, let's-cuddle-up sort of hat.
  "My hat makes me almost as small as you!"
he cried proudly to the mouse.

The tiny mouse sniffed and looked up at the hat.
A slow, miserable tear rolled down his cheek
    "What's the matter?" asked Juice.
    "I'm cold and I have no house to live in. Your hat
looks so cuddly and warm. It would be just the thing
to curl up inside on a winter's night."

    "You want to sleep in my hat?" squealed Juice, horrified.
    "Oh no," said the tiny mouse, "I could not possibly ask
you to be so kind as to give me your hat."

Juice looked at the mouse as he limped unhappily away. It is not easy for little pigs to be generous and Juice did not want to give his hat away, but he decided to do it.

It was **nice**. The mouse kept shaking his hand and saying thank you because, he said, Juice was so **kind**.
"Ah," said Juice, "I am a Very Determined, Brave, Patient **and Kind** Pig and **I Have No Hat**!"

And so, happy, hungry and hatless, Juice the Pig set
off home to find his mum,

his tea

and a new hat.